and I will tell you, as we go,

some things a little one should know.

You see, my little buttercup,
I've learned some things as I've grown up.
Oh yes, I've learned a trick or two
and I can pass them on to you.
Three simple rules that you will find
are useful things to bear in mind.

WOOF!

IT'S YOUR WORLD NOW!

can you find me in every picture?

This, like everything, is for Catherine.

PAVILION

Pavilion team:
Neil Dunnicliffe, Harriet Grylls, Anna Lubecka

Text and illustrations:
© Barry Falls 2019

First published in the UK in 2019 by Pavilion Children's Books, 43 Great Ormond Street, London, WC1N 3HZ. An imprint of Pavilion Books Company Limited. The moral rights of the author and illustrator have been asserted. All rights reserved. No part of this publication may be reproduced, stored in a retrieval ... photocopying, recording ... 3654100. 10 9 8 7 6 5 ... td, China.

FSC
MIX
Paper from responsible sources
FSC® C104723

05486134

Little one, come walk with me,

there is so much for us to see,

The first of them is rather fun,

I call it...

LESSON
NUMBER

The world is full of
marvellous things!

Like cats that purr
and birds that sing.

Like ships that sail
the ocean blue
and trees and lakes
and mountains too!

Like brightly
coloured butterflies.

Like rock and roll
and lullabies.

Like midnight feasts
and morning cuddles,
autumn leaves
and splashy puddles.

Chocolate cake and ice-cream sundaes,
never-ending-summer-fun-days.

As for you,
my bouncing ball,
well you can truly have it all.
Yes, you can set the world alight,
my child-so-small,
your future's bright.

See kids like you, undoubtedly,
can choose whate'er they want to be
and be that thing, quite splendidly
– the best *that-thing* in memory.

Perhaps you'll be a
film director,

cook
or vet
or tax inspector.

Acrobat
or deep sea diver,

judge or nurse or race car driver.

With hard work and application
you can rise to any station.

President,

or CEO!

There's nowhere that
you cannot go.

Perhaps you'll fly
amongst the stars,
to start a colony on Mars,
or build the world's
first time machine
and go where
no-one's ever been.

You'll test the limits!
Break the rules!
You'll have no fear!
You're no-one's fool!
You'll venture into
worlds unknown.
The power of you
is yours alone.

Oh how I wish that I could say

that's all you need to learn today.

But I could never lie to you,

alas, it's…

LESSON NUMBER 2

Things won't always go your way.

You cannot *always* win the day.

You will not *always* be the best

or finish first or ace the test.

You will not *always* live the dream

or be the cat to get the cream,

or claim the prize for every game

or hear the people chant your name.

In fact, sometimes, they'll lecture you

on how to speak and what to do.

They'll say...

No, you can't have it all,
oh little one, you're *very* small.
Just know your place and be content.
You'll never be a president.
That kind of thing is just for dreams
– it's not as easy as it seems!

Wait a second, is it true?
Is that what I am doing too?
Do I believe, because I'm tall,
my little one, I know it all?

Perhaps the best thing, on reflection,
is to go your *own* direction.
Lessons that have worked for me
may not apply to you, you see.

Your life is *yours*, and yours alone,
and you'll discover on your own
just who you are and why you're here.
But even so, I'll persevere...

...for one last lesson,
then we're done.

It is the most important one.
I've saved the best to last, you see,
it's time for...

LESSON
NUMBER

3

The only thing
you need to know.
Above all else,
I love you so.

Of this, at least, I have no doubt.

The rest, I can't say much about.

So go and play and live and learn.

It's *your* world now.

This is *your* turn…

...to think and ask and make and do.

This world is magic, just like you!

So paint a picture.
Climb a tree.
Pretend to be a bumblebee.
Break a record.
Make a thing.
Scream and shout
and dance and sing.

Do all of this,
or none at all.
It's up to you!
Kid, it's your call.

Just remember,
as you go,
the *single* thing
you need to know.
The golden rule
that bears repeating,
true as long as
my heart's beating.
From your head
down to your toe,

no matter what...

I love you so!